Stan
and the
Toilet
Monster

by Steve Shreve

Marshall Cavendish Children

For Lauren

Text and illustrations copyright © 2011 by Steve Shreve

Marshall Cavendish Corporation, 99 White Plains Road, Tarrytown, NY 10591
www.marshallcavendish.us/kids

Library of Congress Cataloging-in-Publication Data
Shreve, Steve.
Stan and the toilet monster / written and illustrated by Steve Shreve. —
1st ed.
    p. cm.
Summary: When Stan's pet chameleon, Fluffy, who was accidentally flushed
down the toilet by his dog, encounters a growth formula flushed by mad
scientist Doctor Rrhea, disaster follows and only Stan, with his best friend
Larry, can save the day.
ISBN 978-0-7614-5977-4 (hardcover) — ISBN 978-0-7614-6086-2 (ebook)
[1. Chameleons—Fiction. 2. Sewerage—Fiction. 3. Scientists—Fiction. 4.
Schools—Fiction. 5. Humorous stories.] I. Shreve, Steve, ill. II. Title.
PZ7.S559149St 2011
[Fic]—dc22   2011001233

The illustrations are rendered in pencil and inked in Photoshop.
Book design by Anahid Hamparian
Editor: Marilyn Brigham

Printed in China (E)
First edition
10 9 8 7 6 5 4 3 2 1

mc **Marshall Cavendish**
Children

Contents

Prologue

It happened on that fateful day late last summer.

Stan was getting ready for bed; and as always, he brought along his loyal pet chameleon, Fluffy. Fluffy liked to sit on top of the cool porcelain toilet.

While Stan brushed his teeth, the family dog, Mr. Snuggles, slinked into the bathroom.

Probably wants a drink of water from the toilet, Stan thought.

It was pretty gross, but Stan had learned that it was best to stay out of Mr. Snuggles's way if you didn't want a fresh set of teeth marks on your keister.

Mr. Snuggles wasn't interested in water, though—he was interested in a tasty little after-dinner snack.

Mr. Snuggles leaped up, knocking Fluffy into the toilet with a loud **SPLASH!**

Things might have turned out okay if Mr. Snuggles hadn't hit the flush lever on his way down.

WHOOSH! Gurgle, gurgle, gurgle.

Mr. Snuggles snarled and bolted from the room.

"FLUFFY!" Stan shouted. "NOOOO!"

Stan began to furiously plunge the toilet, but it was no use. Fluffy was gone.

chapter 1

The Not-So-Natural

Once it became obvious that Fluffy wasn't coming back, Stan slowly stopped thinking about her. Instead he put all of his energy into playing baseball with his friends in his front yard. They mostly played there because Stan's dad hated mowing the lawn and encouraged anything that would kill the grass.

And because when Stan and his friends played anywhere else, they usually weren't allowed back.

So far, they had ruined Coleman's dad's prize-winning petunia patch, accidentally destroyed the toolshed in Charlie's backyard, and they were still sworn to secrecy about what happened at Artie's house.

Stan loved baseball even though he wasn't very good at it. Today he was stuck playing left field out between the garbage cans and the garden gnomes. He was bored—no one *ever* hit a ball out this far.

Just as he was starting to doze off, Stan heard the loud *crack* of a bat. He looked up and saw the baseball.

I wonder why the ball is getting bigger . . ., he thought.

Then it hit him.

THWACK! The ball bounced off his forehead and rolled across the street.

Stan's friends quickly dropped their gloves, raced over . . .

... and ran right past Stan. They chased the baseball to the sewer drain, where it disappeared.

"Do we have any more balls?" asked Miles.

"That was the last one," said Ray. "Mr. Snuggles ate the rest."

The boys stood around wondering what to do.

"Someone could go after it," Miles said.

"What about the monster that's supposed to live down there?" asked Charlie.

"I heard it's half man, half fish," said Coleman.

"I heard it's a sludge monster that mutated from all the stuff people flush down their toilets," said Artie.

"Quit being ridiculous," said Ray. "Everybody knows it's a giant alligator."

Stan walked over, rubbing the lump on his forehead.

Maybe he was brave. Maybe he didn't believe in the monster. Maybe he wasn't thinking clearly after being hit in the head with a baseball.

"I'll go," he announced. "I'll go down into the sewer and get our ball back." Silence fell over the group.

Stan turned to his best friend, Larry. "Let's go, Larry."

"What? Why me?" asked Larry. Larry could be a bit of a wimp sometimes.

"You owe me," said Stan. "Remember last week when I helped you study for the math test?"

"But I failed that test," Larry pointed out.

"You still owe me," Stan said.

"Oh, all right," said Larry.

chapter 2

A Foul Ball

The first thing they noticed was how dark it was. The second thing they noticed was the smell.

"Pee-yew!" said Stan.

"Sorry," said Larry. "I had chili for lunch today."

Larry turned on the key chain flashlight he kept for emergencies and looked around.

Stan held his nose.

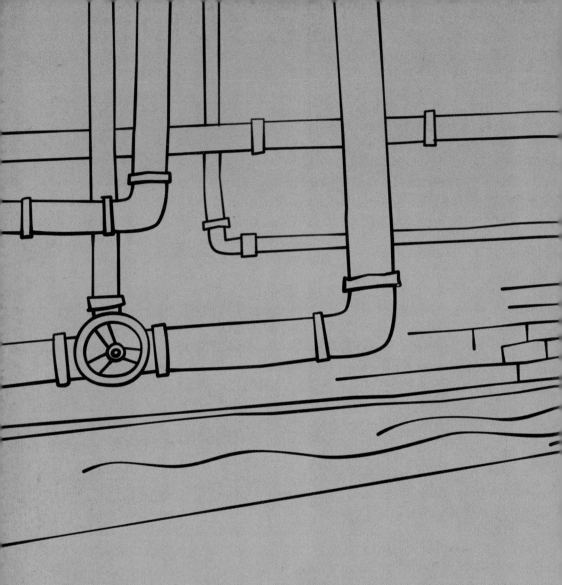

"There it is!" Stan said, pointing. "We sure are lucky the current didn't carry it away."

Stan and Larry watched as the current carried the baseball over the edge.

"Darn! Maybe we should try to get another ball from Mr. Snuggles," Larry suggested.

"Things didn't go so well for the last person who tried that," Stan reminded him.

"You mean Lefty?" asked Larry.

Stan nodded solemnly.

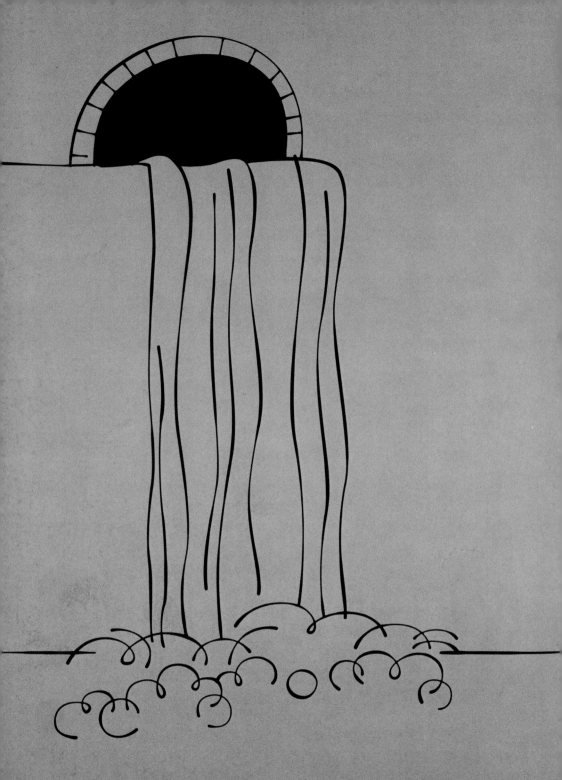

"Come on—let's just see if we can get it." Stan climbed over the ledge and dropped down.

Larry followed, landing waist deep in the swirling water. The new matching socks and underwear his grandmother had given him were completely ruined. He made a face.

"Quit being such a chump," said Stan.

The two boys chased the ball through the long, dark, winding tunnels of the sewer. Every time they got close, the ball would get carried away in the sewer's strong current.

Finally, the ball got lodged in a corner. "I can get it!" Stan yelled to Larry.

But as he reached out for the ball, it slipped through a large crack in the wall.

Stan turned to Larry. "It looks like we're going in."

"Well, if you think it's safe . . .," said Larry.

Stan and Larry squeezed through the crack into a huge underground cavern. Stalactites hung from the ceiling, water dripped down the slimy walls, and the floor was cracked and uneven. It was almost completely dark.

They peered around and saw what looked like a large pile of mud. The ball sat on top, covered in muck.

Stan picked up the ball. "Gross. I really hope this is just mud," he said.

"Wait—how did the ball get up there?" Larry's voice trailed off as something moved in the shadows.

Stan saw it, too.

"Stay calm," Stan whispered. "Now is not the time to panic."

The thing in the shadows started to growl.

"Okay," said Stan, "*now* it's time to panic!"

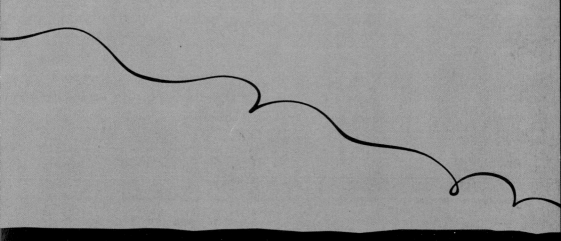

Stan and Larry did the only thing they could think to do. They ran like crazy back the way they came.

After a few minutes they stopped, their chests heaving.

"I think we lost it," Stan panted.

"I think we need to get in better shape," Larry said.

They didn't notice the dark figure silently creeping up behind them.

"Did you hear something?" Stan asked.

They slowly turned . . .

chapter 3

Hammer Time

The monster reached up and pulled the mask off its face. "Howdy, boys." Stan and Larry found themselves looking at a man.

"What a relief," said Stan.

"It's a good thing my underwear is already wet," Larry added.

"Who are you?" Stan asked the man.

"Jack Hammer," he replied, holding up an official-looking badge. "Department of Pest Control Services."

"Why were you wearing that gas mask?" asked Larry. "You scared us pretty bad."

"*I* wasn't scared," said Stan.

Larry gave Stan a disgusted look.

"If there's one thing I've learned about being in the sewers," said Jack, "it's that they sure don't smell like daffodils."

"I noticed that, too," Stan said.

Larry nodded gravely.

"Are you here to get rid of the monster?" Stan asked.

"I'm here to take care of the rat problem."

"But I didn't see any rats," said Stan.

"Not anymore—I sent down a bunch of cats to chase them out."

"I didn't see any cats, either," said Larry.

"Well," said Jack, "when they wouldn't leave, I had to resort to more drastic measures."

Larry, his eyes wide, said, "You don't mean—"

"That's right. Now I'm here to get rid of the poodles."

"Poodles?" said Larry.

"How?" asked Stan.

"By observing their behavior, learning their ways, and eventually becoming a trusted member of their pack. Speaking of poodles," said Jack, "you should probably leave before they figure out you're here."

"Why—are they dangerous?" Larry asked.

Jack looked serious. "Well, they've been down here a while, and I think they're getting pretty hungry."

There's nothing meaner than a hungry poodle, Stan thought. Even Mr. Snuggles avoided poodles, ever since his scuffle with old lady Ferguson's poodle, Portia, over a half-eaten liverwurst sandwich.

"We *would* leave," explained Stan, "but I think Larry may have taken a couple of wrong turns back there."

"Hey!" Larry complained.

"Just follow this tunnel for about a mile," Jack said. "You should see a ladder. It will take you up to a manhole in the middle of Calamity Avenue."

"Thanks," said Stan.

"A whole *mile*?" grumbled Larry.

Stan and Larry started to trudge through the tunnel.

"I can't believe we have to walk all the way home dripping wet," whined Larry.

"It's not so bad," said Stan. "After wading around in all that water, we won't have to take baths tonight."

"Umm," Larry said, "you do realize that it's sewer water we've been walking in?"

"Whatever," said Stan. "At least we've got our ball."

chapter 4

Meanwhile, on
Calamity Avenue . . .

An hour had passed, and Stan and Larry's friends were getting restless.

They were about to head home when Miles heard a loud scraping sound. "Hey, do you guys hear that?"

"Look!" Artie called.

They all turned and watched as the manhole cover in the middle of the street began to slide.

"Something's coming out of the sewer!" hollered Miles.

"It's the monster!" yelled Charlie.

"Alligator!" Ray cried.

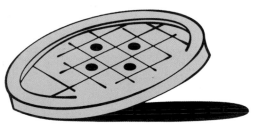

Now most people would have run screaming at the very thought of a monster climbing out of the sewer. But the boys of Calamity Avenue were made of tougher stuff. That and, well, they *really* wanted their baseball back.

The boys crowded around the manhole.

Coleman hoisted a baseball bat as the manhole slowly slid open . . .

"Put down that bat!" said Stan, climbing out. "It's me, Stan!"

"And me, Larry!" Larry added as he pulled himself out.

Coleman reluctantly lowered the baseball bat.

"Where were you?" asked Charlie.

"We thought the monster got you," said Artie.

"Where's our baseball?" asked Ray.

"Here it is." Stan reached into his pocket and pulled out the slimy, dripping ball.

Everyone gathered closer for a better look (but not too close—the smell was pretty awful).

"I don't know what that thing is," said Ray, "but it's NOT a baseball."

The boys gasped.

Now that he was looking at it in the sunlight instead of in the nearly pitch-black cavern, Stan wasn't so sure it was a baseball, either.

"You know," Stan said, "it seemed a *little* too heavy."

Larry leaned in. "Yeah, and it's the completely wrong shape, size, and color," he added helpfully.

"If it's not our baseball," asked Charlie, "then what exactly *is* it?"

"Maybe it's something valuable," offered Coleman. "Like a giant pearl buried hundreds of years ago by our town's pirate founding fathers."

"It could be a magical crystal ball left behind by fairies," said Artie. "Or maybe by elves."

Ray was not convinced. "I think it's a rock."

Stan had to admit that it did look more like a rock than a baseball.

"Hey, guys, maybe we could take it to Doctor Rrhea," suggested Larry. "He's a scientist. He could run some tests or something."

"Yeah," Ray said. "A *mad* scientist."

"Great idea, Larry," Stan said, ignoring Ray. "Let's go."

The doctor's house was all the way across town, and it was getting late. Stan and Larry hopped on their bikes and sped away.

chapter 5

The Doctor Is In

The closer to Doctor Rrhea's house Stan and Larry got, the more nervous Larry became. "Are you sure about this? I mean, Doctor Rrhea is pretty weird."

"He's okay," said Stan. "He used to work with my dad teaching science at the community college. That was before the explosion, of course—but how was he supposed to know that mixing pop rocks and cola would level the science building?"

It was almost dark by the time Stan and Larry arrived. They left their bikes on the lawn and cautiously approached Doctor Rrhea's house.

"Are you sure this is the place?" asked Larry. "It doesn't really look like the kind of place a mad scientist would live."

It was true—the house was a cottage with white shutters and window boxes full of gerbera daisies.

Stan walked up the front steps and rang the doorbell. The notes of "La Cucaracha" rang out from inside the house.

The front door sloooooowly opened. A tall, gaunt figure peered out at them.

"If you're here to sell me magazine subscriptions," he said, "I'm not interested."

"We came about this." Stan held up the dripping, foul-smelling rock.

Larry just stood there, pale.

"We were wondering if you could look at it. With you being a scientist and all," Stan quickly added.

Doctor Rrhea sighed. "Very well. Let's take a look in my laboratory."

"If anyone can determine what you have there, it's me," the doctor pronounced as he escorted the two boys through the house. "I am, after all, the inventor of twelve-day underpants, edible tape, and giant brussels sprouts."

"Big deal," Stan whispered to Larry. "I've been wearing *my* underpants for a *lot* longer than *that*."

"Giant brussels sprouts?" Larry said. "Yuck."

"Believe it or not, people don't really seem to care for brussels sprouts as much as you would think," said Doctor Rrhea.

"You don't say," Stan said.

"It was such a failure that I ended up flushing the brussels sprouts *and* the growth formula down the toilet."

"Isn't that bad for the environment?" asked Stan.

Doctor Rrhea shrugged. "What's the worst that could happen?"

They finally reached Doctor Rrhea's laboratory at the back of the house. It looked a lot like a kitchen.

Doctor Rrhea took the rock from Stan. Next he put the strange object through a series of scientific tests. He held it up to his ear and listened. He held it up to his nose and sniffed. Then he tapped it carefully with his index finger. Finally, he licked his finger for a taste test.

Stan and Larry exchanged a look.

"Hmm," said Doctor Rrhea, his eyes narrowing. "Where exactly did you say you found this?"

"The sewer," answered Stan.

"I really wish you had told me that earlier," the doctor replied, wiping his mouth on his sleeve. "Please excuse me while I go brush my teeth."

Doctor Rrhea was gone for quite a while. Getting the taste of sewer out of your mouth can take some time.

When he returned, he found that Stan and Larry were getting ready to leave.

"Going somewhere?" the doctor asked.

"Well, since you can't figure out what this is . . ." Stan held up the rock.

The doctor snatched it away. "You know, boys—if I could run some more tests, I'm sure I could find out what this is. Why don't you leave it with me for a few days?"

Secretly, the doctor had figured out *exactly* what the rock was. And he had his own nefarious plans for it.

"That's okay," said Stan, prying the rock from the doctor's grip. "I think I'll bring it to school tomorrow. Maybe Mrs. McGillicuddy will know what it is."

Doctor Rrhea walked Stan and Larry to the front door, trying to convince them to leave the object with him. But it was no use. Stan would not give it up.

Doctor Rrhea sat in his laboratory, upset that he'd allowed something so valuable to escape his grasp.

He needed to get it back. He thought and thought until he had the perfect plan. "I'll show those other professors at the community college—call *me* a weenie, will they?"

chapter 6

A Night to Remember

Stan should have been exhausted after the day's excitement. But that night he couldn't fall asleep.

He kept thinking about showing his rock to his teacher the next morning. If that creepy Doctor Rrhea didn't know what it was, maybe she would.

The smell coming from the rock was completely foul.
Worse than toe cheese and sweaty baseball jersey combined.
The odor was so bad, in fact, that not even Mr. Snuggles could
come near it. And Mr. Snuggles smelled like he'd been rolling
around in a garbage dumpster for the last two weeks. Which,
of course, he had.

Stan finally nodded off into a restless sleep. But not for long. Later that night, *something* woke him up. It was a horrible, scraping sound, and it was coming from outside.

Maybe it's a burglar, Stan thought. *Or an axe-wielding maniac*. He got up to take a look.

He opened the window and peeked out. He didn't see anything unusual going on, but it was pitch-black outside, so it was hard to tell.

Weird, thought Stan. *That noise sounds familiar—where have I heard it before?*

Stan finally went back to bed, and he fell asleep as soon as his head hit the pillow.

The next day, Stan woke up late and had to run to catch the bus. If Stan missed it, his dad would make him walk the mile and a half to school, even though he drove past the school on his way to work. His dad said it built character.

Stan knew something wasn't right as soon as he stepped out the front door. The mailbox was up in a tree. The birdbath was upside-down in the middle of the driveway. The garden gnomes were broken and scattered all over the yard. But what confused Stan the most were the huge V-shaped holes all over the lawn.

At least his dad would be happy that he wouldn't have to mow.

Stan didn't have time to investigate. He ran to the bus stop, looking over his shoulder every once in a while, just in case.

He arrived at the bus stop with a few minutes to spare. Larry was already there, waiting.

"Hey, Larry!" Stan said as he trotted up. "Did anything strange happen at your house last night?"

"Now that you mention it," said Larry, "at dinner my mom served me a pork chop that bore a striking resemblance to Abraham Lincoln."

"*That's* not what I'm talking about!"

"Well, *I* thought it was pretty strange."

"No, no, no. I mean like weird noises. I heard something in my yard last night. And when I woke up this morning, it looked like a bulldozer had come through."

"Really?" Larry said, looking worried. "You don't think it has anything to do with the sewer monster, do you?"

"I hadn't thought of that," said Stan.

"Or maybe it was a raccoon going through the garbage looking for food," Larry continued. "My dad puts bricks on top of the lids to keep critters out."

"The only things in our garbage last night were leftovers from dinner. Even the raccoons won't eat my mom's cooking."

"It still could've been raccoons," Larry said, trying to convince himself.

"Larry, you've eaten at my house," Stan remarked as the school bus pulled up to the curb.

"You have a point," said Larry.

Meanwhile, across the street, hidden behind a hedge, Doctor Rrhea crouched with a pair of binoculars.

He must have the specimen, the doctor thought as he watched Stan get on the bus. He absently scratched at his ear. *And after I get it back, I will show those buffoons at the community college just how wrong they were about my work!*

The doctor scratched his arm. *Why am I so itchy?* he wondered.

He looked at the branches that were stuck to his clothing and counted the leaves. One, two, three ... *Uh, oh. It's poison ivy!*

"Bah! What else could possibly go wrong?" he bellowed.

It was probably a bad decision to ask that question out loud.

Mr. Snuggles, who just happened to be lurking nearby, came around the hedge. He began to growl and bare his teeth.

"Good doggy," the doctor said. Then he turned and ran.

chapter 7
School Daze

Stan wanted to talk to Mrs. McGillicuddy before anyone else got to class. He jumped off the bus as soon as it came to a stop. There was no running allowed in school, so he made sure the coast was clear before he sprinted down the hall.

"Mrs. McGillicuddy!" Stan yelled, bursting through the door. "Look what I found!"

"Quiet in the classroom," Mrs. McGillicuddy said to Stan, not for the first time.

"Okay," Stan said, his voice slightly quieter. "But I want to show you something I found."

Mrs. McGillicuddy, still on her first cup of coffee for the day, was shocked awake. Stan almost never showed an interest in her teaching—or anything that didn't involve baseball.

"What is it?"

"I don't know. I was hoping you could tell me."

Mrs. McGillicuddy took the rock from Stan and gave it a close look.

"Interesting," she said. "Where did you say you found it?"

"In the sewer."

"I really wish you had told me that sooner," said Mrs. McGillicuddy, reaching for the box of antiseptic wipes she kept on her desk.

"Why don't you put this somewhere safe until after class?" she said, handing it back to Stan. "Preferably in a place where it won't ... disturb the class."

"Disturb the class?"

"With the smell, Stan."

"Oh," said Stan. "Right." He carried the rock, oozing and dripping, back to his desk.

The bell rang, and Stan's classmates came streaming in.

Larry took his seat next to Stan. "Hey, Stan," he whispered, "I think I see something outside the window."

Stan looked. "I don't see anything."

"Maybe it's the monster," said Larry, his eyes wide.

"You think?" said Stan, turning toward the window again.

Mrs. McGillicuddy addressed the class. "All right, everyone. Please hand in your homework."

The students pulled out their notebooks and began passing their papers forward.

"Homework?" said Stan. In all of the excitement yesterday, he had completely forgotten.

This is going to be a long day, Stan thought.

Meanwhile, Doctor Rrhea had finally gotten away from Mr. Snuggles and had arrived at Stan's school.

He was standing outside, hoping to spot Stan or, better yet, the specimen. This wasn't easy since Mrs. McGillicuddy's classroom was on the second floor. But he could see through the window by standing on top of a dumpster behind the cafeteria.

From his perch at the window, he watched Stan slip the specimen inside his desk.

This is better than I had hoped, Doctor Rrhea thought. *As soon as everyone leaves for lunch, I'll sneak in and take it.*

But when Larry turned and looked out the window, Doctor Rrhea was taken by surprise. He quickly leaned to the right, out of Larry's view. Suddenly he lost his balance and landed headfirst in the dumpster. *"Nooo!"*

"Blech," he groaned. He threw a salisbury steak that was stuck to his head over the side.

He laid there recuperating while leftovers from the previous day's lunch seeped into his underwear.

chapter 8
Food Fight!

That morning's lesson was on integers. Stan didn't understand any of it. Although, to be fair, he really wasn't paying attention—he just couldn't stop thinking about his rock ... and the monster.

Could the monster have followed them out of the sewer, ruined his yard, and then come to school?

Finally the bell rang.

Yes! he thought. *Lunch!* Lunch was Stan's favorite thing about school. Especially today—it was meat loaf Wednesday.

He slipped the rock into his pocket and headed to the cafeteria.

At the lunch table, Stan told everyone about his adventures in the sewer the previous day. His classmates hung on his every word about monsters, mysterious caves, and sewer poodles. Everyone, that is, except Judy.

"Well, I don't believe any of it, Stan Hankie," she said.

Judy had been Stan's enemy ever since kindergarten, when she told the class that he still slept with a teddy bear. Sure, it was true, but Stan would never forgive her. They'd been bitter rivals ever since.

"Oh yeah? Then how do you explain this?" Stan pulled the rock from his pocket, spraying everyone with reeking goo.

Stan's classmates stared at the rock, amazed.

"Ooh," someone said.

"Aah," said someone else.

"I think I'm going to be sick," said Artie.

"Eew," said Miles, pushing his tray away.

Coleman didn't say anything and took another bite of his sandwich.

Stan passed the rock around. "Careful," he said. "No one knows what it is. It could be dangerous—it could be deadly poisonous, or explosive, or ..."

"Or a rock," said Judy, looking smug. "Besides, if it was something special, wouldn't you be worried that the monster might crawl out of the sewer to get it back?"

"Nope," Stan replied, trying to look more confident than he felt.

Larry, however, panicked at the suggestion. His eyes bulged, and milk sprayed out of his nose.

"Gross," Judy muttered.

"I don't think it can get out of the sewer," argued Stan. "It would be too big to fit through the manhole."

"The sewer overflow pipe behind the school is definitely big enough for a monster to fit through," Judy pointed out. "I bet it's on its way here right now."

"The monster is coming?" said Miles, who tended to be excitable.

"Boy, I'm sure glad I'm not you, Stan," said Coleman. "Or you," he added, turning to Larry. Larry was looking a little green.

"It's probably coming to get this *thing* back," Artie said, realizing that he was holding the rock.

Suddenly, no one wanted to be holding Stan's rock.

"I don't want it!" cried Artie, tossing it to Miles.

"Don't give it to me!" Miles yelled, immediately passing it to Coleman.

"I don't want the monster after me!" Coleman said, sending it off to the closest person he could find.

Pretty soon everyone was yelling and trying to get rid of the weird object.

And that's when total pandemonium broke out. The great East Stumptonville Elementary School Cafeteria Food Fight of '98 looked like a tea party compared to this.

Food trays fell, spilling milk and meat loaf everywhere. Chairs were knocked to the floor. A spork flew through the air, narrowly missing Mrs. McGillicuddy. Someone dropped Stan's rock, and it left a long, gooey trail as it rolled across the cafeteria table.

And then it was all over, almost as quickly as it had begun.

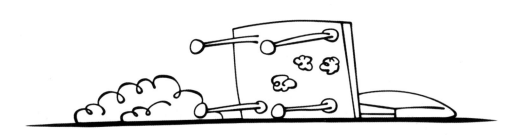

"That's quite enough!" shouted Ms. McGillicuddy.

She pointed to the rock, which had rolled to the end of the table. "Mr. Grimes, would you please dispose of this *thing*?" she asked.

Mr. Grimes, the school's janitor, came over and picked it up. "Where did this come from?" he asked. He held it to his nose and took a big sniff.

"The sewer," said Ms. McGillicuddy.

Mr. Grimes considered this for a moment, then shrugged. He headed out the back door to the dumpsters behind the cafeteria.

Mr. Grimes avoided the half-eaten salisbury steak that Doctor Rrhea had thrown out earlier. "Darn dog," he grumbled, thinking Mr. Snuggles was the culprit. "Always making a mess that *I* have to deal with."

He went over to a dumpster and tossed the rock inside.

He never noticed the huge shadow that crept up behind him.

Earlier...

A short time before, Doctor Rrhea had been sitting in the dumpster, cleaning salisbury steak gravy out of his underwear and wondering how he was going to get into the school to steal the specimen.

That was when, without warning, something bonked him squarely on top of the head. Something *hard*. The doctor looked around to see what had hit him. He couldn't believe his eyes.

He wouldn't have to find the specimen after all—it had come to him!

Doctor Rrhea reached over and snatched the specimen from a pile of curdled tapioca, rotting banana peels, and rancid salisbury steak.

"It's mine!" he shouted, holding the specimen in his hand. "This will show those eggheads at the community college just how important I am!"

chapter 9

Something Comes Up after Lunch

Stan's class was back at their desks, listening to Mrs. McGillicuddy's lecture on the virtues of proper lunchroom etiquette.

Stan had the sneaking suspicion that she was directing most of her comments toward him. He couldn't believe she'd had his rock thrown out like that.

Then, right in the middle of Mrs. McGillicuddy's speech, Mr. Grimes came bursting through the door.

"There's a monster on the loose!" He stood in the doorway, a thick, puddinglike slime dripping onto the floor below him.

No one knew how to react. Things like this just didn't happen every day at East Stumptonville Elementary School.

"Would you like an antiseptic wipe?" Mrs. McGillicuddy offered him the box from her desk. She looked skeptical.

"Nah, I'm good," he answered, wiping his dirty hands on his filthy shirt.

"What kind of monster was it?" Charlie asked from the back of the classroom.

"Was it half man and half fish?" asked Coleman.

"Sludge monster?" asked Artie.

"It was an alligator, wasn't it?" asked Ray.

"Don't know," Mr. Grimes replied. "The low-down critter snuck up behind me. I didn't see anything 'til I was halfway down his gullet."

Larry was more than a little freaked out. "He tried to eat you?" It was bad enough being hunted by a sewer monster, but it was worse knowing it could eat you, too.

"How did you escape?" Stan asked.

"I fought my way out! That, or it spit me out because it didn't like the taste of my aftershave."

Stan turned to Mrs. McGillicuddy. "Can I go with Mr. Grimes to see where it happened?" He couldn't help but feel *partly* responsible for all the trouble. Plus, he wanted to find out what happened to his rock.

Mrs. McGillicuddy didn't really think there was a monster but knew that if she didn't let Stan go, he would fidget all afternoon.

"You can go," she replied. "*If* it's okay with Mr. Grimes."

"Eh, why not?" Mr. Grimes shrugged.

"Come on, Larry," Stan said.

Larry shook his head. "Uh-uh. No way."

"Why not?" Stan asked. "Afraid you'll get your under-pants wet again?"

Larry blushed.

The trio arrived at the dumpster. "It was right here," the janitor said. But nothing was there now.

"I don't see any monster," whispered Stan.

"Maybe it's invisible," Larry whispered back.

"Don't be ridiculous," whispered Stan.

"Why are you two whispering?" shouted Mr. Grimes. He couldn't hear too well because his ears were filled with monster mucus.

Maybe the monster heard him, because suddenly there it was. The monster had come for them!

They gazed up at the towering beast.

"It's humongous!" said Mr. Grimes.

"It's horrible!" said Larry. "Although strangely familiar."

"It's ... Fluffy," said Stan.

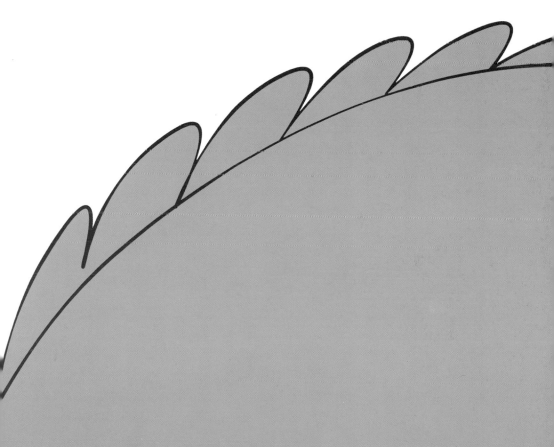

chapter 10

Fluffy

"Fluffy?" asked Mr. Grimes.

"My pet chameleon," answered Stan. "But I lost Fluffy over a year ago. . . ."

"How did you lose something that big?"

Fluffy swiveled an enormous eye to look at them. She took a slow, deliberate step forward.

"Fluffy used to be a lot smaller," Stan said.

Stan, Larry, and Mr. Grimes began to retreat, never taking their eyes off Fluffy. They only made it a couple of steps before they knocked butt-first into something cold, hard, and slightly sticky.

They were trapped—backed into the dumpster at the end of a short, dark alley and now face-to-face with a very large, very angry, and (quite possibly) very hungry toilet monster.

"Guess we're done for," said Mr. Grimes.

"I'm too young to be eaten by a giant chameleon!" cried Stan.

"These pants are ruined," said Larry, frantically rubbing at his backside with a handkerchief. "My mother is going to kill me!"

"I'm not so sure she's going to get the chance," Stan said.

"I don't get it," said Stan. "I saw Fluffy get flushed down the toilet."

"That explains how she got into the sewer," said Mr. Grimes. "But how did she get so BIG?"

Stan started to remember something—it seemed important, but he couldn't quite put his finger on it. Then he got it.

"Brussels sprouts! Fluffy must have eaten Doctor Rrhea's brussels sprouts growth formula!"

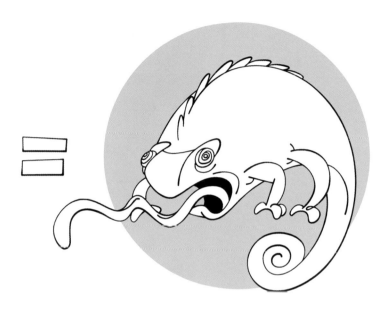

BOOM!

Fluffy took another gigantic step forward.

"Sorry, boys," said Mr. Grimes. "Looks like you're dinner."

"Us?" said Stan. "What about you?"

"Already spit me out once, remember? Feel bad for you two, though."

Stan closed his eyes and prepared for the worst. "Nice knowing you, Larry," he said.

Larry couldn't answer because he was too busy hyperventilating.

Fluffy swiveled her other eye toward them and opened her mouth.

Just then a loud shout broke the silence. "Hey, ugly!"

"What?" Mr. Grimes shouted back.

"Not you. I'm talking to the giant toilet monster."

Fluffy, more annoyed than anything else, turned . . .

... and faced Jack Hammer and an army of miffed poodles.

"Attack!" Jack ordered.

High-pitched yipping filled the air as the poodles surged forward. But they were no match for a cranky four-thousand-pound chameleon who had just had her feelings hurt.

CRACK! A poodle named

Peanut chipped her front tooth while nipping at Fluffy's tough, leathery toes.

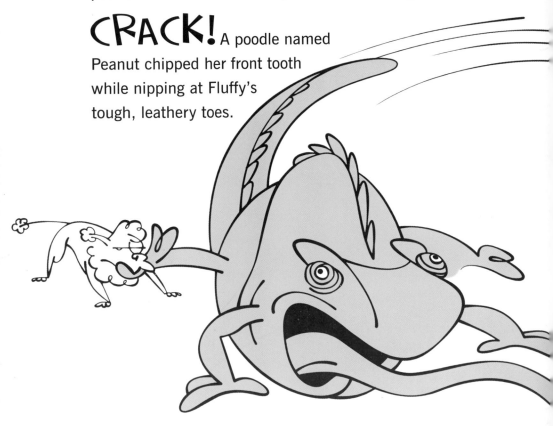

WHACK! Fluffy hit Miss Prissy—three-time winner of the East Stumptonville Dog Show (most well-groomed category)—with her massive tail, sending the dog flying.

THWAP! Fluffy's extralong tongue hit Handsome Pierre, covering him in a thick layer of mucus.

Fluffy let loose, swatting poodles left and right.

Stan watched as poofy fur, diamond-studded dog collars, and pink hair ribbons flew through the air.

But that wasn't the worst of it. . . .

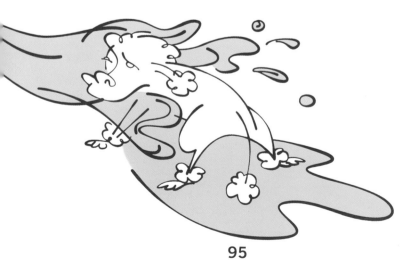

Fluffy opened her mouth and released a belch so foul it could only have come from a giant sewer monster.

The few remaining poodles gagged, coughed, and passed out from the unbearable stench.

"Gross," said Stan. "That could have been us."

"Quick!" Jack shouted at Stan, Larry, and Mr. Grimes. "Over here!"

They darted out of the alley while Fluffy was distracted.

"Good thing you came when you did," said Stan. "But how did you know we were being attacked?"

"I didn't," replied Jack. "That varmint came out of the sewer last night, wrecking everything in sight. You should see what she did to the town cesspool—*not* pretty. These poodles and I have been tracking her all night."

"Why?" Stan asked.

"Somebody has to stop her," Jack said. "And I *am* a pest control professional."

chapter 11

Fluffy vs. the Greater Metropolitan Area

Fluffy lumbered across the parking lot. She missed most of the cars—except for a 1975 lime-green Chevy Vega with an I Brake for Unicorns bumper sticker and three hubcaps.

KA-RUNCH!

She crushed that car perfectly flat with one giant step, her massive tail scattering bits and pieces behind her.

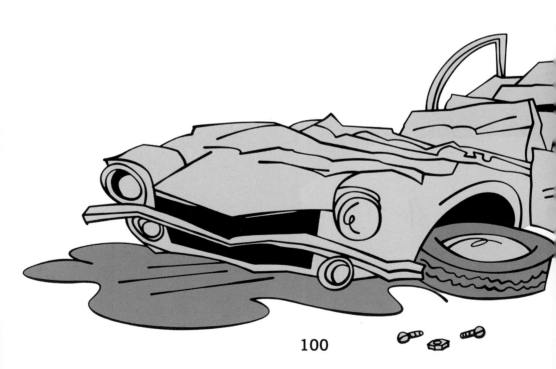

Stan, Larry, Jack, and Mr. Grimes heard the crunch of metal and glass and sprinted around the corner.

"My car!" shouted Mr. Grimes. "I only had three payments left!"

Stan tried to make him feel better. "Things could be worse," he said.

"How could things possibly be worse?" Mr. Grimes asked.

"Your car could have caught fire," Stan offered.

Just then Mr. Grimes's Vega burst into flames.

In the distance they could see Fluffy running through the playground, demolishing the jungle gym and swing set as she went.

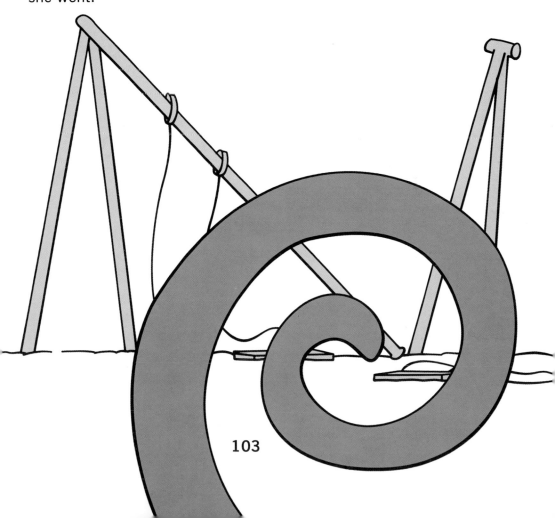

"We have to do something!" Stan said to Jack.

"You're right," said Jack. "I think I have a few hand grenades left over from that mouse infestation back in '02."

"But you can't blow up Fluffy!" Stan cried.

"Sure I can. Should take two, maybe three grenades tops."

"That's not what I meant," said Stan. "Fluffy was my pet. Can't we just set a trap or something?"

Jack thought about this and seemed to come to a decision. "Everybody! To the Pest Control Action Van!"

Stan and Larry ran to Jack's van.

Mr. Grimes stayed behind, picking up pieces of his car.

"Shotgun!" said Stan, hopping into the front seat.

"Darn," said Larry. "I get carsick in the backseat."

Jack climbed behind the wheel.

Stan saw Fluffy disappear around the corner of the school, heading toward the fields. "She's getting away!" said Stan. "Let's go!"

"How can we follow her?" asked Larry. "She's running across the soccer field."

"We'll take the side roads and head her off before she reaches a populated area," said Jack. "Buckle up."

Jack put the van in gear and peeled out of the parking lot, tires squealing.

It was a good thing Stan had on his seatbelt. The van swung wildly from side to side as Jack sped down a series of narrow streets and alleys, keeping an eye out for any sign of Fluffy. He even managed to get the van up on two wheels at one point.

Larry, who had nothing to hold on to in the backseat, bounced around like a Ping-Pong ball. "Ugh. I think I'm going to be sick."

Something metallic rattled in the back as the van flew over a speed bump at sixty miles per hour.

Stan held onto the dashboard for dear life. "You're sure those hand grenades are stable, right?" he asked.

"Pretty sure," said Jack. "Why?"

"No reason," Stan said, bracing himself for an explosion.

Jack finally brought the van to a screech-ing halt in the middle of Main Street.

"What do we do now?" asked Stan.

"We wait," said Jack.

Larry didn't say anything. He was too busy getting sick out the van window.

They didn't have to wait long before Fluffy appeared from between two buildings and faced the Pest Control Action Van.

Jack put the Action Van in gear and hit the gas, heading right for Fluffy.

The giant chameleon let out a yelp and ran down the main street of East Stumptonville as fast as she could.

Which wasn't very fast. Chameleons, even giant ones, aren't speedy creatures. What followed was quite possibly the slowest car chase in history.

Fluffy disappeared as she changed colors to blend into her surroundings. This wasn't easy, considering that the surroundings were brightly painted shops and restaurants on a downtown street.

Stan was on lookout while Jack drove. Larry moaned from the backseat. If Stan squinted, he could just make out Fluffy against the background. Plus, the destruction she left behind was a dead giveaway.

"Hey!" shouted Stan. "There she is."

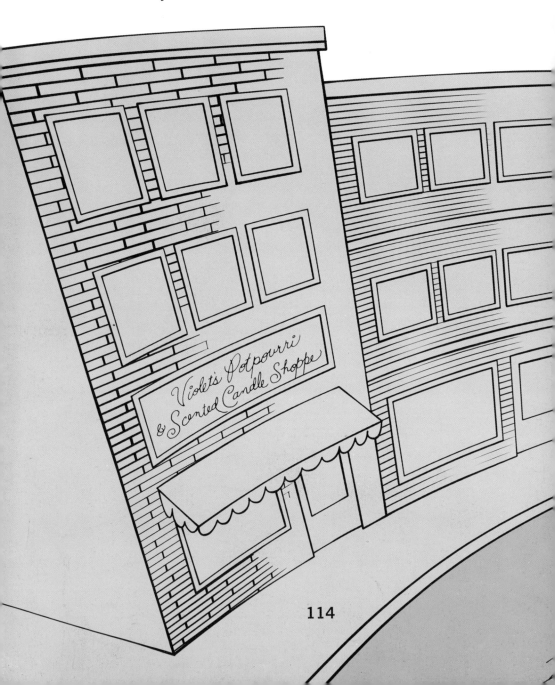

Violet's Potpourri & Scented Candle Shoppe

Jack jerked the wheel to the right and pulled the Action Van alongside Fluffy. Using his van, he herded the chameleon toward Violet's Potpourri & Scented Candle Shoppe.

Fluffy turned purple.

Jack nudged her with the nose of the van toward Rose's Discount Flower Outlet, where she turned a bright pink.

ROSE'S DISCOUNT FLOWER OUTLET

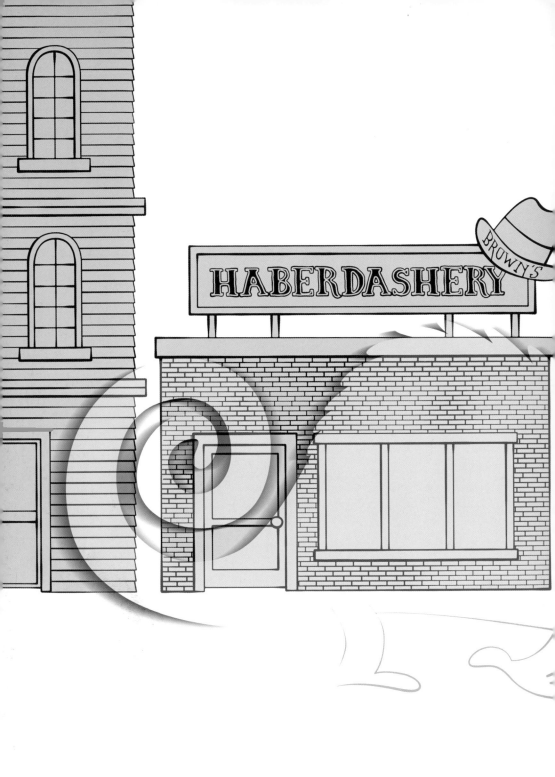

Next, he cut her off in front of Green's Hardware Emporium, where Fluffy turned a lovely shade of chartreuse as she tried to blend in.

After that she had to run past Brown's Haberdashery, turning an appealing shade of . . . well, brown.

Jack managed to keep pace with the runaway chameleon.

Fluffy made a last-ditch attempt at escape and veered left toward a side street. Jack swerved to cut her off.

Fluffy had no choice but to continue down Main Street past the MacHaggis Kilt Emporium. The front of the store was decorated in tartan plaid.

That stopped Fluffy cold. She made a strange sort of gurgling noise, twitched, and passed out.

"What happened?" asked Stan, jumping from the van.

"Everybody knows chameleons can't turn plaid," explained Jack.

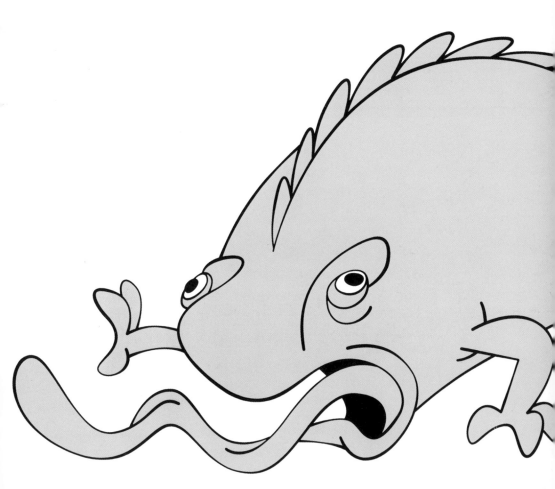

119

chapter 12

Stan: The Man with a Plan

"Why did Fluffy leave the sewer in the first place?" Stan wondered aloud.

"She's probably after her egg," Mr. Grimes said from behind them. He came walking up, carrying what looked like a muffler. The chase had been so slow that he was able to catch up on foot.

"Egg?" said Stan. "What egg?"

"I think he means your rock," said Larry.

"Ohhhh ...," said Stan. It slowly dawned on him that Fluffy wasn't on a rampage for no reason—the rock was really her egg, and she wanted it back.

Stan felt terrible. He had to get Fluffy's egg back to her. "Jack, fire up the van," he said.

Jack climbed into the Action Van and started the engine.

"Larry, you're with me and Jack," said Stan. "We might need your flashlight."

Before Larry could complain, Stan turned to Mr. Grimes. "Can you stay here and watch Fluffy?" he asked.

"Let me get this straight," Mr. Grimes said. "You want me to watch a four-thousand-pound lizard with giant claws, razor-sharp teeth, and anger management issues?"

"Right," Stan said.

"No problem," Mr. Grimes replied. He sat down on the curb next to Fluffy and watched the Pest Control Action Van pull away in a cloud of blue smoke.

Stan, Jack, and Larry arrived back at the dumpster behind the school.

"Larry, hop in the dumpster and take a look around," Stan said.

"Why me?" said Larry. "My mother will freak out if she finds out I've been crawling around in there."

"Okay," said Stan. "How about you climb in, and I'll owe you one?"

Stan's reasoning made sense, so Larry climbed in. "Eew, salisbury steak," he moaned.

Larry surfaced a short while later, gasping for breath. "Ugh, it smells like onions and feet in here."

"Never mind that," said Stan. "What about the egg?"

"Nothing yet," Larry said glumly.

Stan was about to tell Larry to keep looking when they heard frantic yelling from the front of the school.

Larry climbed out of the dumpster, and the trio raced around the corner. There they saw one of the most horrifying things ever.

What they saw—or rather *who*—was Doctor Rrhea.

Fleeing with the egg, he had climbed the chain-link fence that separated the school parking lot from the street. Unfortunately, his underwear had gotten caught on the top as he jumped down. Now he was experiencing what had to be the world's biggest wedgie.

"Ouch," said Jack. "That's gotta hurt."

"I wouldn't wish that on my worst enemy," Larry added.

"Is he wearing twelve-day underpants?" Stan asked.

"Hey!" said Stan. "He has the egg! I guess you didn't need to search the dumpster after all, Larry."

Larry opened his mouth to say something but was cut off by a loud *RRRIIIIIPP*!

"Ah, man," said Stan. "I think someone cut the cheese."

But it wasn't a fart—it was the elastic waistband on Doctor Rrhea's underwear tearing free. The doctor landed in a mud puddle on the other side of the fence.

He stood up slowly, underpants sagging.

"Ha!" he laughed. "Now I'm safe on this side of the fence, and there's nothing you can do to stop me!"

"Stop you from doing what?" asked Stan.

"Hatching the egg, of course. I will raise my own giant chameleon and finally get my revenge on those fools at the community college who laughed at my inventions! Ha-ha-ha-ha-HA!"

"At least he seems happy," Larry commented.

chapter 13

Fluffyzilla

"Now, if you'll excuse me," Doctor Rrhea said, walking away, "I have more important things to doooooo."

Doctor Rrhea suddenly rose ten feet in the air.

"You don't see that every day," said Stan.

Fluffy lifted the doctor high above the ground.

Apparently, turning plaid only stuns chameleons temporarily.

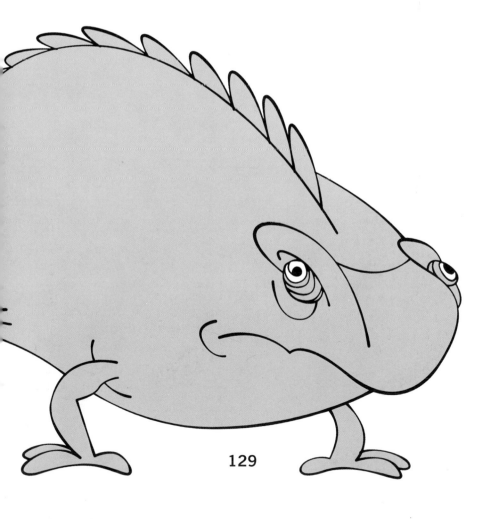

Fluffy let out a loud roar and went crashing through the fence, with Doctor Rrhea hollering the whole way.

Mr. Grimes ambled up a few seconds later.

"I thought you were keeping an eye on her," said Stan.

"She must have snuck away when I nodded off," Mr. Grimes said. "Don't worry. She'll calm down once she gets her egg back."

That was when Doctor Rrhea dropped the egg. Lucky for him, the chameleon didn't notice.

Fluffy used her chameleon toe-gripping power to scale the wall of the school, pulling out chunks of brick as she climbed.

When Fluffy stepped onto the roof, the school was evacuated. The students were in an uproar. Nothing this exciting ever happened at school. The last time there was an evacuation, Mrs. McGillicuddy had smelled something she thought was poisonous gas. It turned out to be an egg salad sandwich that Stan had left in his desk over the weekend.

Coleman stared up at Fluffy. "If she doesn't come down, I bet we won't have school tomorrow."

"Maybe we'll get the whole week off," said Miles.

"I heard that after ten minutes they have to let us go home for the day," said Ray.

"But we'll miss the history quiz this afternoon." Artie frowned.

The other boys looked at Artie.

Ray opened his mouth to speak again, then stopped.

Tanks were rolling into the parking lot. Artie tried to speak but was drowned out by the deafening sound of helicopters swarming in the sky.

It was the East Stumptonville Unincorporated Township Auxiliary Volunteer Militia reporting for duty. The regular town militia was unavailable due to old lady Perkins's cat being stuck in a tree. A pack of wild poodles had chased her up there.

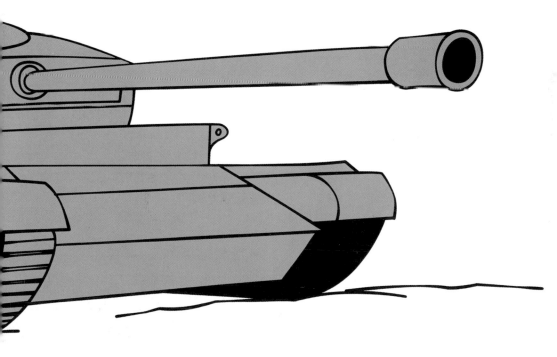

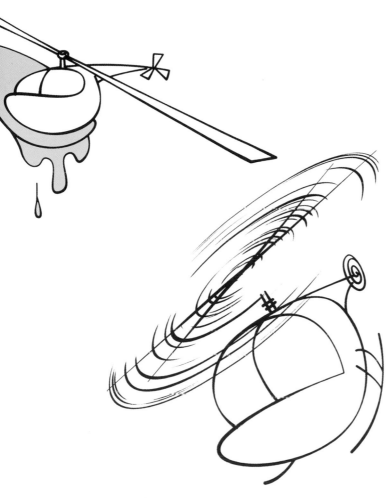

Fluffy stood her ground, the roof of the school cracking under her awesome weight.

Helicopters buzzed around Fluffy, but she swatted them down one by one with a swipe of her giant clawed foot.

And those were the lucky ones.

The unlucky ones were hit by her incredibly fast, incredibly slimy tongue.

A helicopter dropped out of the sky covered in wet, dripping, sticky glop.

"Dang," muttered the sergeant who was in charge. "That's going to come out of my paycheck."

The sergeant picked up a bullhorn and began to bark orders.

"Ready the bazookas!" *TAP, TAP, TAP*. "Is this thing on?"

Stan ran up. "But that will destroy the school!"

All of Stan's classmates cheered (some of the teachers, too). If the school was obliterated, they'd probably get the rest of the year off.

"Please give us a chance," pleaded Stan. "You don't have to blow up the school."

Stan's classmates booed.

"She just wants this." Stan showed the sergeant the egg.

"Why?" he said. "It's broken."

"Huh?" Stan looked at the egg, puzzled.

"It's got a crack in it."

Sure enough, there was a thin, jagged crack running up the side of the egg. "It must have happened when Doctor Rrhea dropped it."

Stan thought he heard a faint scratching noise coming from inside the egg. He held it up and looked at it—something looked back. Then the shell fell away.

Stan was holding a baby chameleon! A *giant* baby chameleon.

"Aack," it squawked.

"Let's get you back to your mama," Stan said.

Stan handed Fluffy Junior to Larry. "C'mon, Larry, you take Junior."

"Yeeouch!" Larry cried, as the little chameleon bit his thumb.

"Listen," said the sergeant. "I can't let you go up there. It's too dangerous."

"Please?" asked Stan.

"Okay. But only for five minutes. After that we blow up the school."

Stan sprinted up the stairwell that led to the roof, with Larry right behind him. He had done more running in the last two days than he had all year. "After this, I'm not exercising for a month," Stan said.

Larry would have answered, but he was having his own problems. Fluffy Junior had sunk her claws into Larry's shoulder and was holding on tightly. Her tail was also wrapped around his neck. Larry huffed and puffed his way up the stairs.

Stan burst through the door to the roof. "Fluffy! It's me, Stan!"

Fluffy did *not* look happy.

Stan backed up a step. "Larry," he whispered. "Give her Junior—quick. Larry?"

Larry wasn't there.

"Good Fluffy. It's me . . . your old pal Stan."

Giant cracks appeared in the roof as Fluffy took another step forward and opened her mouth.

Uh-oh, thought Stan. Fluffy stepped closer . . .

Larry finally came through the door, gasping for breath.

"What took you so long?" said Stan. "I was almost chameleon food."

"Can't ... breathe ...," Larry wheezed.

Junior relaxed his grip on Larry's throat and ran to Fluffy. Fluffy was so happy that she dropped Doctor Rrhea—right into a patch of wet tar that was left over from some roof repairs Mr. Grimes had made.

"Great," said Larry. "How do we get her down?"

chapter 14

What Now?

Convincing a giant chameleon to get off the roof of a two-story elementary school is harder than one might think.

Stan tried calling her. Then he tried pulling her. Then he tried pushing her, careful to avoid the general butt area. He even tried bribing the chameleon with $1.67 and a jelly doughnut he found in his pocket.

But no matter what Stan tried, Fluffy wouldn't budge.

Out of ideas, Stan, Larry, and Doctor Rrhea walked down to the parking lot.

"There's only one thing to do now," said Stan.

"Bazooka?" asked the East Stumptonville Unincorporated Township Auxiliary Volunteer Militia sergeant.

"More plaid?" suggested Jack. "Or maybe polka dots."

"Abandon the school?" said Larry.

"What? No!" Stan said. "I know the one thing that Fluffy's scared of. It's risky, and probably a little gross, and also dangerous. Very dangerous. As a matter of fact, some of us might not make it back. Now, who's with me?"

Everyone seemed to be really busy. Someone pushed Larry forward.

"Thanks, Larry," Stan said. "I can always count on you."

Larry didn't argue; it would be no use. Besides, his clothes were already ruined—what else did he have to lose?

Stan and Larry didn't exactly like the idea of going back to the dumpster. But they had one last trip to make.

Stan crept around the corner.

"C'mon, Larry. Yeah, he's here."

And there was Mr. Snuggles. He had never looked happier. He was rolling around in the dumpster, covered in a week's worth of school lunch leftovers.

It took some work, but Stan and Larry finally managed to get Mr. Snuggles out of the dumpster, up the school stairs, and onto the roof. Stan pulled while Larry pushed. In the end, Stan ended up bribing the dog with the $1.67 and jelly doughnut in his pocket. Mr. Snuggles scarfed it all.

Fluffy might have been larger than a city bus, but she still recognized her old enemy when she saw him.

And Mr. Snuggles recognized *her*. He drooled.

Fluffy turned and ran, making sure not to leave Junior behind. The already damaged roof fractured and split under Fluffy's massive bulk as she tried to escape.

Fluffy and Junior ran to the other side of the roof as Mr. Snuggles chased after them. They were backed into a corner.

Mr. Snuggles's stomach growled. Jelly doughnut or not, he was still hungry. The dog crouched down, ready to pounce.

But just as he leaped, the battered roof finally gave way completely under Fluffy's colossal weight.

Mr. Snuggles's bared teeth missed Fluffy by mere inches as she and Junior tumbled to the ground far below.

Fortunately, they landed unhurt in the cafeteria dumpster, surrounded by a swarm of buzzing flies.

And if there's one thing a chameleon can't resist, it's a tasty, plump, juicy fly.

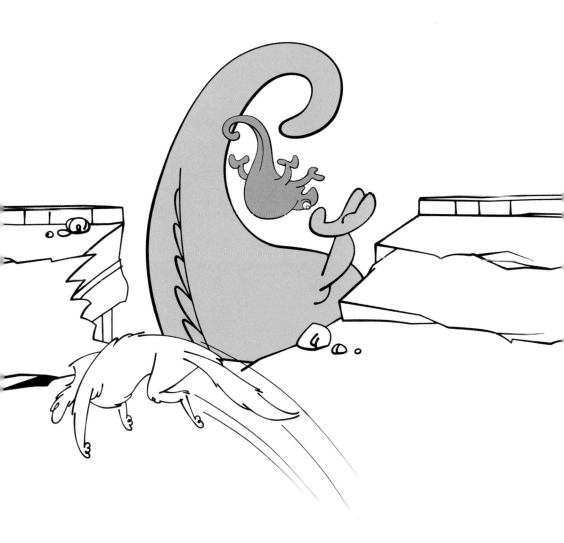

Epilogue

Eventually things quieted down in East Stumptonville.

Jack thought about taking Fluffy and Junior back to the sewer, but they seemed happy enough living behind the school, with an endless supply of flies to eat.

With the sewer finally free of rats, cats, poodles, and giant chameleons, Jack joined a traveling circus with his trained poodle act.

Doctor Rrhea was sentenced to one thousand hours of community service, repairing the damage done to Main Street. Sadly, even though he had discovered (and probably helped to create) not one but two giant chameleons, his colleagues at the community college still thought he was a weenie.

Mr. Grimes made lots of money repairing the school and was able to put a down payment on a newer car. A 1978 Plymouth Duster with an easy, eight-year payment plan.

Stan went home and finally played a game of baseball with Larry, Coleman, Miles, Charlie, Artie, and Ray. They used a chewed-up baseball Stan stole from Mr. Snuggles when he wasn't looking.

Larry continued to be a good (but wimpy) friend.